This little story required the work of many people. First, my wife Mickie who witnessed the whole event and kept me straight on the facts. She even made me coffee from time to time. Of course, you can not see the work that Lauren did to illustrate this book without believing that I have found a genius. She helped, as well, with formatting and editing. I also submitted this book to the Western Suburbs Writers group who gave many hours of excellent advice. And, last but far from least is that, always smiling, incredibly helpful Susan Stradiotto who is an author in her own right. I am proud to call her a friend. She edited my work and then got this printed.

This is a little book I know, but no book is simple. They all require love and devotion.

–DON DELINE

DON'T MESS WITH Mama!

To Alice~
Your mom would
protect you just like
mother Loon!

A TRUE STORY BY **DON DELINE**

ILLUSTRATED BY **LAUREN WILLIAMSON**

Legend has it that, in 1950, some loon relatives of mine had two chicks. We lost both of the parents in one afternoon. A local man, who saw the whole thing rowed out to the dead couple and discovered there were two chicks swimming around frightened and now alone. We loons keep our chicks on our backs from the day they hatch, but often, the chicks are not visible at a distance. On that day, the hunters probably didn't know there were little ones on the backs of the parent birds, although it wouldn't have made any difference to them. The two boys with guns did the killing just for fun. They weren't interested in what they had done. Only that they could do it.

The man who found the little ones had no idea how to care for two orphaned chicks, so he placed them in a box and headed for town. The loons ended up with two young girls named Pat and Char who lived at Lake Hubert during the summers.

The legend goes on that those two ten-year-old girls loved the loon chicks like they had hatched the two themselves. Every day, the girls seined for minnows. They took their morning catch to some rocks and smashed them up to feed the baby chicks. It took a few days for the little balls of feathers to trust the girls, but before long, the baby loons were having trouble telling the difference between loons and people. The girls took as good care of them as any parent could have and spent most of every day playing with them in the lake. At night, they put them in a big box with a net on top, and the loons slept well, considering that loons never leave the water once they hatch—sort of like fish.

We loons mate for life, and we return to our original place of birth as long as it remains hospitable. And ever since Pat and Char took my ancestors in, Lake Hubert has been just that. I have no idea how many generations in my family landed here and had chicks. All I know is that those girls started a tradition that has been unbroken for nearly seventy years…and prosperous years, they have been.

L ouise, that's my mate, and I are, right this minute, circling down to claim our little nest on Eastman's point for another year and try to have our sixth chick.

I am Larry, and Louise and I have been coming here for over four years in spring when there is little or no ice on the lake.

Those nice people on Eastman's point have cleaned the nest and have it ready for this year's new member of the family. A real craftsman built that nest, because it is just what we like. It has a bottom made of reeds that keep the eggs just above the water level. That makes it easy for us to climb into because our feet aren't very good at climbing or walking long distances. Over the generations, loon feet have moved from the middle of their bodies to the back, just in front of the tails, because we never walk anywhere but use our feet to propel ourselves in the water.

The nest floats and is anchored off shore so that no skunks, raccoons, cats, and snakes will get to our eggs without being seen. There is only one problem with Lake Hubert. The water is so pure and the fish so plentiful that Eagles abound. In fact, as we land, a huge old Eagle named Jody circles overhead, thinking that this will be her year to get our chick. We've seen her grab other chicks and watched them squirm as she took them away in her talons. We've managed to keep our chicks safe for four years, and we'll fight to do so again this summer.

Louise and I make certain the nest is still to our liking and then place a bit of mud in the bottom. We shape the mud to our undersides and let it harden. Louise then lays our eggs. For the next 30 days, give or take a few, we take turns sitting on the nest. When we're not on the nest, we check in at the Lake Hubert buffet for some of the finest Bass and Walleye meals to be found in Minnesota.

It has been a month since we reoccupied the nest. I knew there were two eggs there this year, but they don't always hatch. Most years we're blessed if one egg hatches.

Louise finds me this morning, and her head is held high. On her back she is sporting *two* chicks. This will be a hard year as we'll have to fish for the four of us, but what a treat to have two. My, that missus of mine is a handsome bird and with those two little ones on her back, she looks like a queen to this proud papa. The chicks look like two brown dotted tennis balls and blend right in with the feathers on their mother's back.

I make it a point to sound our special loon call well into the night. Louise has tried to make me hush. She said the people on the lake need to get some sleep, but I couldn't care less about the people around the lake tonight! TWO CHICKS!

One of us fishes while the other guards the little ones. They spend a good deal of time on our backs where we can shield them from the sun with our wings. When we're not fishing, we stay about 3 feet apart, and they swim between us while we watch skyward.

We've learned over the years that, when the chicks are first hatched, there is danger from large fish and turtles who feed on ducklings and loon chicks, but loon chicks start larger than ducklings and quickly become too big for fish and turtles. Loon chicks, on the other hand, become just the perfect size for eagles and hawks. So, my mate and I keep our attention focused each day on what is over head. You have no idea how frightening it is to have the sun blocked out for a second, only to see one of those huge birds circling overhead. Twice within the first two weeks of having the chicks, we had to get side by side with our wings over the little ones and our long, pointed bills aimed skyward. We yelled at the predators as loud as we could, and together, we presented a pretty formidable fortress for them to attack. In both instances, they left us alone, but hawks and eagles have been known to take the chicks right off an unsuspecting mother's back. In addition, once they sight a prey, they remember where it is and check often for an opportunity.

As we feared, Jody Eagle has spied our chicks. She was one of the two eagles we turned away earlier, and she is getting on in years. At her age, Jody prefers to take prey away from other birds who've made the kill than to do the hunting herself. Her age has begun to convince her that any meal should be gotten when the opportunity presents itself, because you never know when the next one will arise. However, she'll wait until we show a weakness. Every day we know she is watching.

Today, the chicks are getting big and are doing beautifully. Louise is spectacular at keeping them close and safe. They will swim off a bit but eventually she calls them back. They know to return quickly, or she will pull a few of their tail feathers out to teach them a lesson. This morning, we are in front of the house in which the Pat of "Pat and Char" used to live. We know it well and feel at home and safe right out in front. There is also a bass bed here, so the dining is scrumptious. A sailboat, about twenty-one feet long, is tethered to a buoy to the north of Pat's house. The sides slant out over the water, leaving a sheltered space to keep our chicks perfectly concealed from dangers above. While Louise and I pretend not to notice, the chicks often swim to the boat and duck up under its sides. If we see them going clockwise, Louise and I head to the boat and go counterclockwise. While it's an old game, they always seem surprised and turn around, quickly hurrying back the way they came.

One of the chicks has decided he wants to live the rest of his life on his mother's back. When she dumps him off, he just crawls back on. The other chick thinks she needs her freedom and takes us on a merry chase swimming away, leaving a wake like a motor boat. Some days, they try to dive like we do. They're still so fluffy and have so little weight that they simply stick their butts up in the air with their heads under water and splash with their wings and feet. It will be a few more weeks before they'll be able to get under the surface.

This morning, I've been out fishing and, as I return, I cannot see the chicks, but Louise appears to be in distress and is swimming very near the sailboat. She's yelling as loud as she can. While I'm desperate to get back and help her, I'm still two or three minutes away from landing. Above, I can see Jody, the Bald Eagle, circling five seconds from the boat and right over Louise's head. Jody has set her wings in dive mode, and there is nothing I can do. I've always admired that wonderful mate of mine and her love of our chicks. She's proving herself again by first tucking the young ones up under the side of the sailboat.

Jody is not in a position to see the chicks being maneuvered to safety, but I can. Once the chicks are hidden, Louise beats the lake surface into a froth with her wings. She continues to scream as loud as possible adding to the confusion of the splashing wings. From the air, it appears to Jody that the chicks or their mother or all three are trying to escape by swimming away from the sailboat. But the chicks haven't moved.

If under attack, a grown loon will either dive or fly off, but the chicks can do neither. Of course, Jody knows that. She's been watching. Fortunately for all of us, Jody hasn't seen the little ones under the edge of the boat, but she does see the commotion. The eagle wrongly determines that the little ones are somewhere inside the sparkling spray of lake water. Before I can blink, Jody dives, talons extended, at the white and silver water geysers below. She knows there is prey in there and she will sort out what she has when she gets back in the air after the kill. Eagles cannot land and then take off from water. Once they have landed in water, they can use their wings like oars and row ashore where they can get out, dry off and then take off. But unlike Osprey, they cannot grab their prey, sit on the water for a second, and then take off. When Jody commits, she must fasten on to her catch and lift it off the water by flaring her wings to gain altitude before resuming the beat.

Jody approaches the churning mass of water and sinks her talons in before she knows what she has. It is too late to turn back. The bad luck for Jody is that she has grasped Louise, not one of the chicks. Weighing between seven and ten pounds, Louise is too big for Jody to lift. Jody only weighs about fifteen. While there is much confusion, it appears that Louise pulls the eagle into the lake with her.

I come down about a minute later, a few yards away. There is nothing to see but black and brown feathers and cascading water from the fight. At this point, Louise's screeching has stopped. There are no bird sounds. Only the sound of two large bodies locked in mortal combat, thrashing the water. Feathers and geysers fly three feet in the air and then…nothing.

The water returns to a calm, placid mirror. There are no bubbles and no sign of life. Instinct tells me not to dive to aid Louise but to stay with the chicks even though the danger from Jody seems to have passed. If I were gone, other eagles might seize the opportunity to grab one of the unguarded chicks. The three of us sit silently and wait. If I had a watch, and of course I don't, I would realize it was only a few minutes, but it seems like hours. There is nothing.

About twenty yards off, a loon appears. It's my Louise. She swims up to us like nothing has happened, and we all four resume our daily activities even though we are extremely excited by all that has happened. Can you imagine how proud I am? How remarkable! Louise accomplished something that no one had ever imagined possible! I feel as if the four of us are invincible.

A loon has bested an eagle!

As is typical of my lady, she never speaks of this. I watch her very closely for the next few days, worrying that she is injured somewhere we cannot see. I also fly over the site of her encounter to see if I can find the carcass of the eagle. Over the coming weeks, Louise doesn't seem to have been seriously hurt, nor did the eagle ever surface. The way I figure it, she wound her up in the weeds of the bass beds so tight she's probably still down there today.

I am one proud papa loon. My lady is amazing.

Our two chicks were flying, diving, and feeding themselves when Louise and I headed south for the winter. Just like Pat and Char's two chicks, our chicks will follow when they have gained a bit more weight. They have excellent built-in GPS systems to guide them to their winter homes. We usually winter in South Carolina, and we hope they join us there. Like Louise and me, they will return to Lake Hubert in the spring.

God looks over little ones, that is true.

Every once-in-a while, however, He can use the help of an exceptional parent, and I am proud to say that my lady is one such parent.

Author's Note

Pat, in the story above, was my sister. She and her friend Char remained friends until Pat passed away in 2009 at age 69. The story, of course, is not really told by a loon, but the facts are true. I witnessed this while sitting in my living room at Lake Hubert in a cabin I built next to my grandmother's cabin. When the eagle and loon hit the water, I ran to the lake and out on our dock. They were struggling not 50 feet from where I stood. The eagle never surfaced and could not have survived. We took our boat out later that day and motored up and down the lake shore but never found the eagle. Today, Lake Hubert's loon population is robust!

From right to left: Don, a friend, Pat, Char.

About the Author

Don Deline was born in Minneapolis, Minnesota and spent many of his childhood summers at Lake Hubert, a lake of 1,287 acres, near Nisswa, Minnesota. He attended Chaska High School and the University of Mississippi where he earned a BBA, Master of Accounting, and Juris Doctor degrees. He graduated in 1968. He married Michele (Mickie) Gardner from Senatobia, Mississippi, and they have one child, Michele, who now lives in London, England. Don spent 26 years in the Judge Advocate General's Corps (the Army's law firm) and four years as the Lawyer for the Senate Armed Services Committee in Washington, DC before becoming a Vice President of a Fortune 100 Corporation. He has a home he built on Lake Hubert next to his grandmother's old house, where he resides six months out of the year. In addition, he goes south during the winter—all the way to Plymouth, Minnesota, a suburb of Minneapolis.

ABOUT THE ILLUSTRATOR

Lauren Williamson is a graphic designer and artist who has lived her whole life in the chilly but beautiful state of Minnesota. She has been doodling and drawing ever since she was old enough to hold a crayon. Besides art and design, Lauren has a passion for animals and animal rescue. She has fostered and rehabilitated 8 dogs, and adopted one— a hairless Chinese Crested dog named Finnick. He can usually be found sitting on her lap while she works. Some of Lauren's favorite memories occurred at the cabin on Lake Hubert, where her family often vacations in the summer.